W9-DIJ-136

POWER CODERS

THE SIMULATED FRIEND

AMANDA VINK

ILLUSTRATED BY JOEL GENNARI

PowerKiDS press™

New York

Published in 2019 by The Rosen Publishing Group, Inc.
29 East 21st Street, New York, NY 10010

First Edition

Illustrator: Joel Gennari
Interior Layout: Tanya Dellaccio
Managing Editor: Nathalie Beullens-Maoui
Editorial Director: Greg Roza

Library of Congress Cataloging-in-Publication Data

Names: Vink, Amanda, author.
Title: The simulated friend / Amanda Vink.
Description: New York : PowerKids Press, 2019. | Series: Power Coders | Includes index.
Identifiers: LCCN 2017057851| ISBN 9781538340172 (library bound) | ISBN
   9781538340189 (pbk.) | ISBN 9781538340196 (6 pack)
Subjects: | CYAC: Computer programming–Fiction. | Morse code–Fiction. |
   Friendship–Fiction.
Classification: LCC PZ7.1.V58 Sim 2019 | DDC [Fic]–dc23
LC record available at https://lccn.loc.gov/2017057851

Manufactured in the United States of America

CPSIA Compliance Information: Batch CS18PK: For Further Information contact Rosen Publishing, New York, New York at 1-800-237-9932

CONTENTS

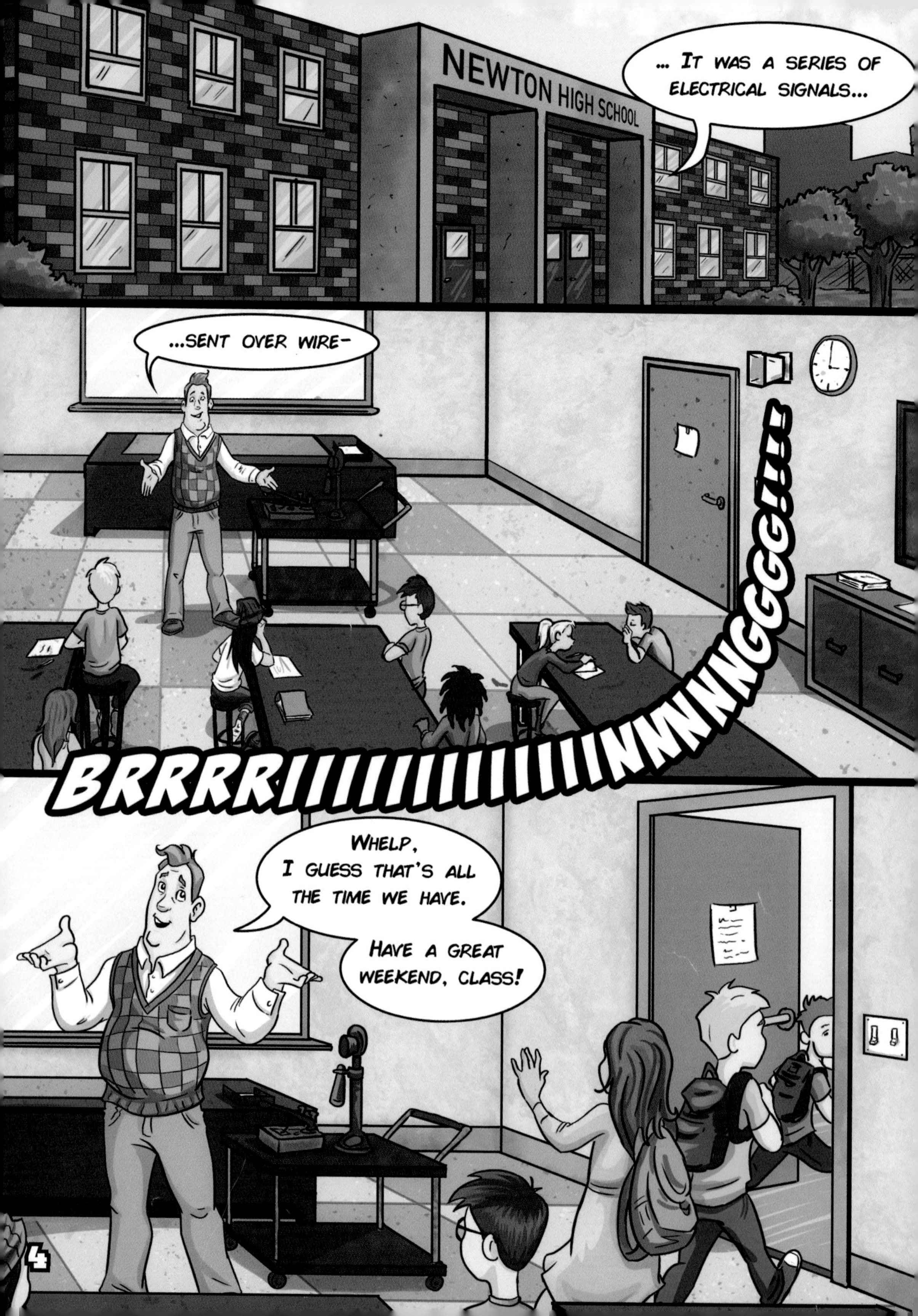
NEWTON HIGH SCHOOL
... IT WAS A SERIES OF ELECTRICAL SIGNALS...
...SENT OVER WIRE-
BRRRRIIIIIIIIIIIIIIINNNNNGGG!!!!
WHELP, I GUESS THAT'S ALL THE TIME WE HAVE.
HAVE A GREAT WEEKEND, CLASS!

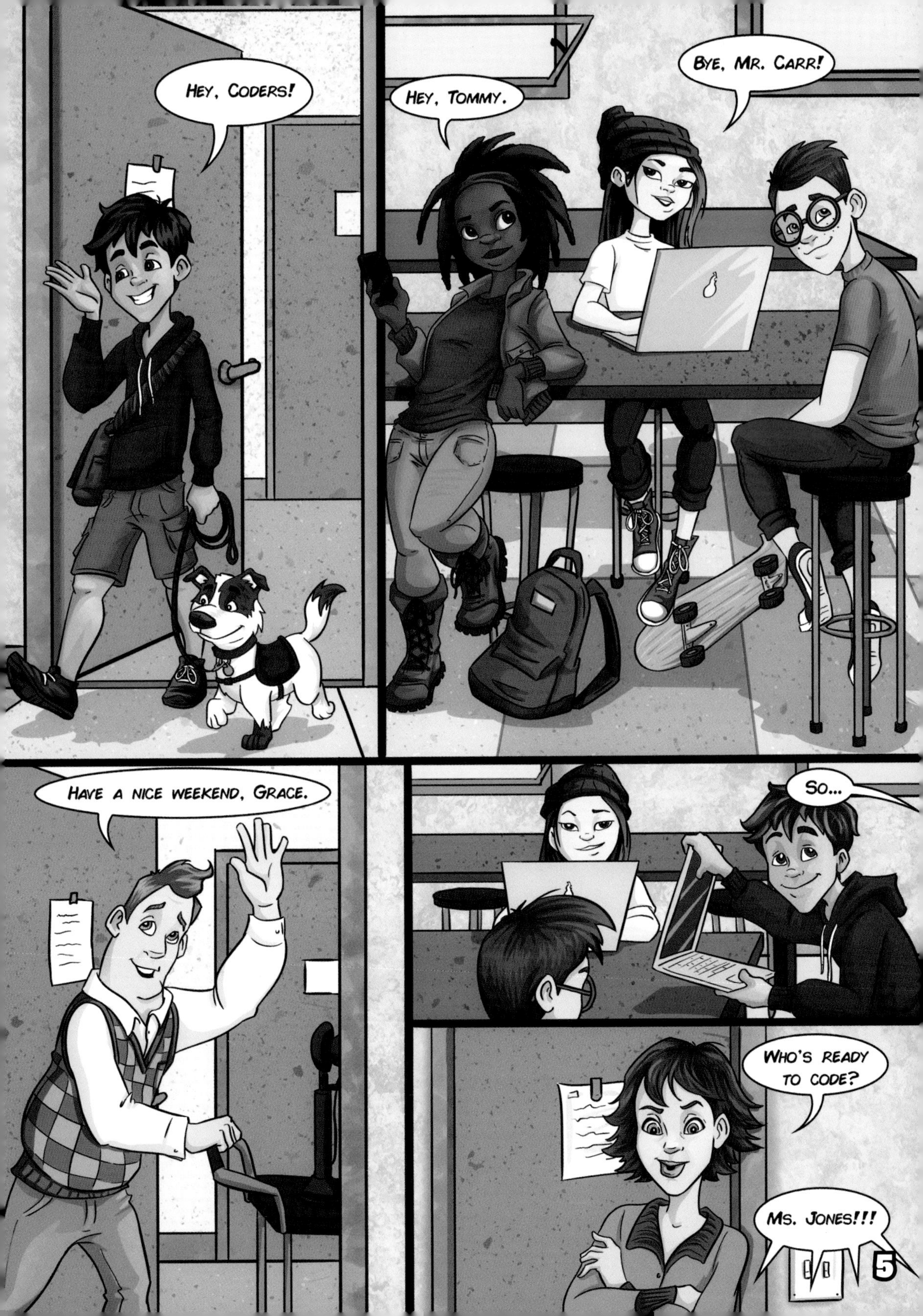
HEY, CODERS!
HEY, TOMMY.
BYE, MR. CARR!
HAVE A NICE WEEKEND, GRACE.
SO...
WHO'S READY TO CODE?
MS. JONES!!!

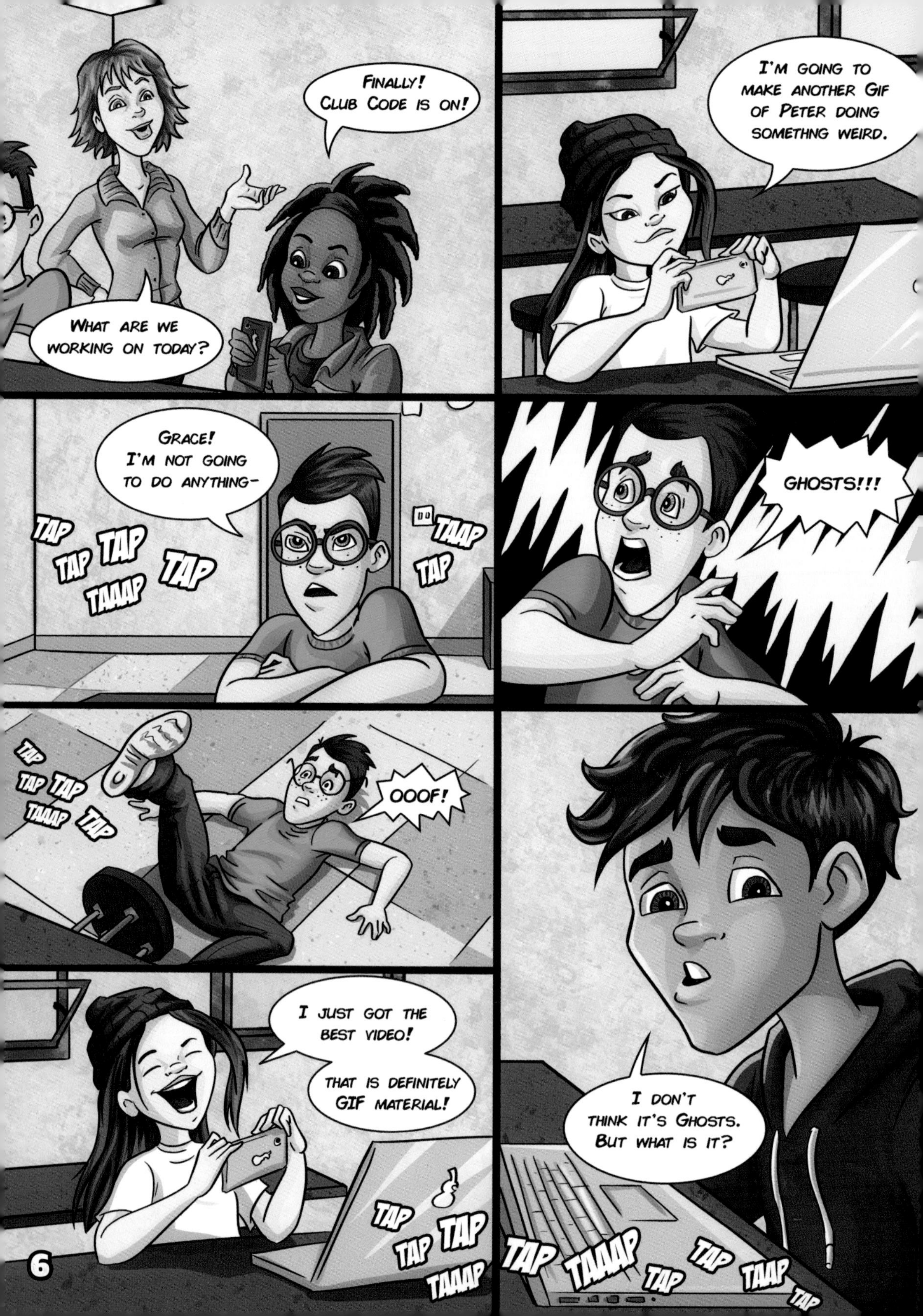

FINALLY! CLUB CODE IS ON!
WHAT ARE WE WORKING ON TODAY?
I'M GOING TO MAKE ANOTHER GIF OF PETER DOING SOMETHNG WEIRD.
GRACE! I'M NOT GOING TO DO ANYTHING-
TAP TAP TAP TAAAP TAP
TAAP TAP
GHOSTS!!!
TAP TAP TAP TAAAP TAP
OOOF!
I JUST GOT THE BEST VIDEO!
THAT IS DEFINITELY GIF MATERIAL!
TAP TAP TAP TAAAP
I DON'T THINK IT'S GHOSTS. BUT WHAT IS IT?
TAP TAAAP TAP TAP TAAP TAP

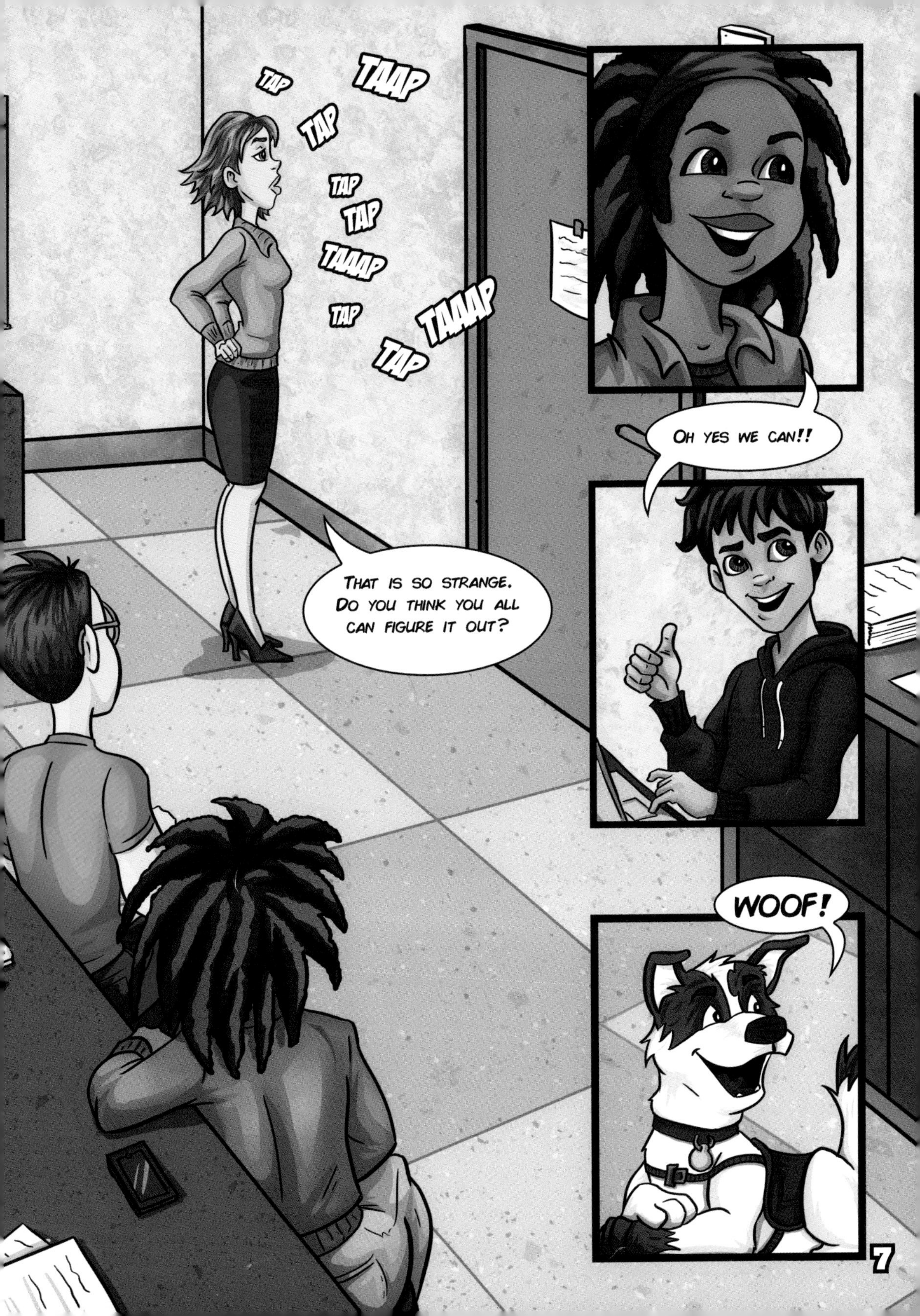
TAP
TAAP
TAP
TAP
TAP
TAAAP
TAP
TAAAP
TAP
THAT IS SO STRANGE. DO YOU THINK YOU ALL CAN FIGURE IT OUT?
OH YES WE CAN!!
WOOF!

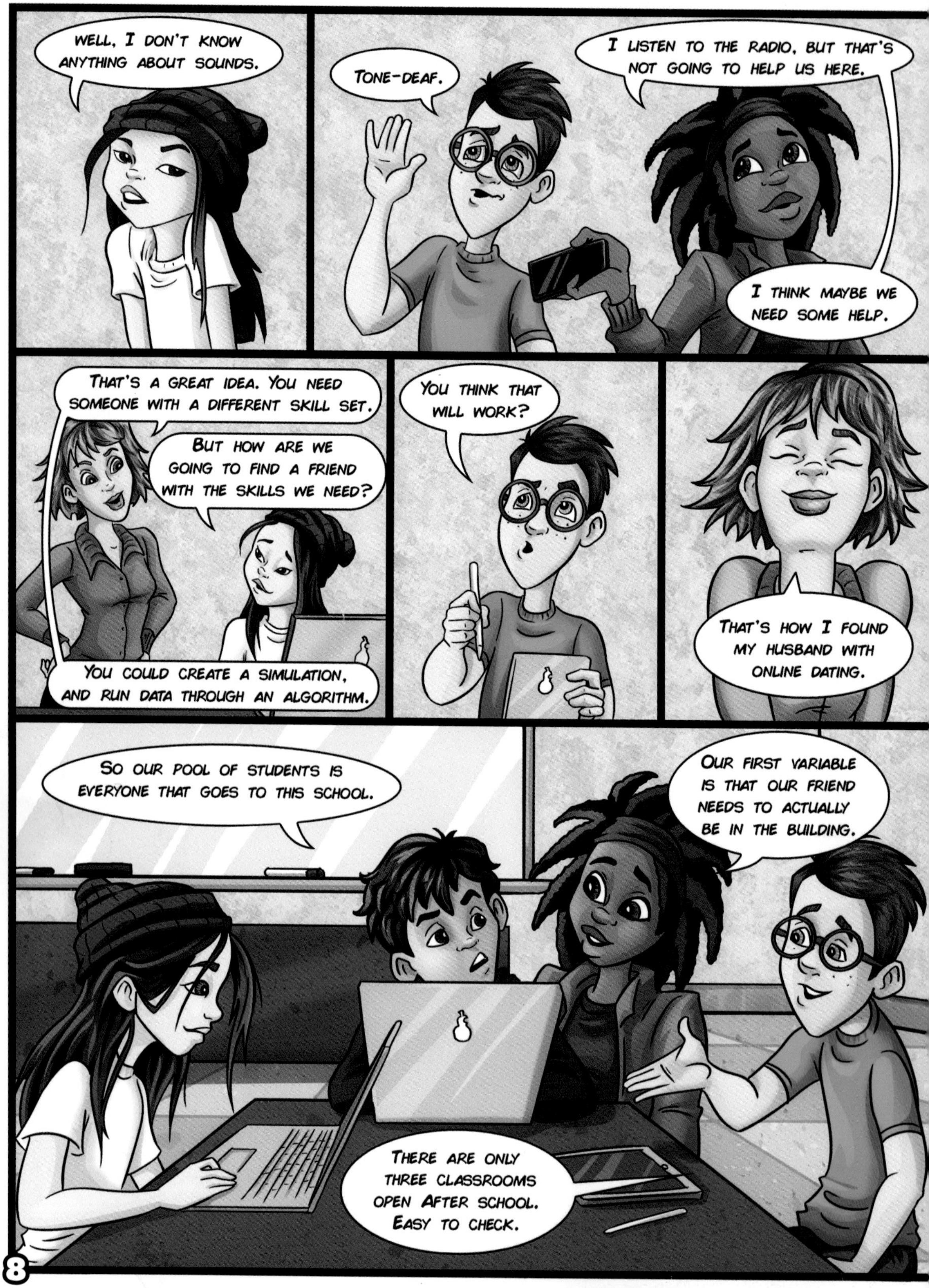
WELL, I DON'T KNOW ANYTHING ABOUT SOUNDS.
TONE-DEAF.
I LISTEN TO THE RADIO, BUT THAT'S NOT GOING TO HELP US HERE.
I THINK MAYBE WE NEED SOME HELP.
THAT'S A GREAT IDEA. YOU NEED SOMEONE WITH A DIFFERENT SKILL SET.
BUT HOW ARE WE GOING TO FIND A FRIEND WITH THE SKILLS WE NEED?
YOU COULD CREATE A SIMULATION, AND RUN DATA THROUGH AN ALGORITHM.
YOU THINK THAT WILL WORK?
THAT'S HOW I FOUND MY HUSBAND WITH ONLINE DATING.
SO OUR POOL OF STUDENTS IS EVERYONE THAT GOES TO THIS SCHOOL.
OUR FIRST VARIABLE IS THAT OUR FRIEND NEEDS TO ACTUALLY BE IN THE BUILDING.
THERE ARE ONLY THREE CLASSROOMS OPEN AFTER SCHOOL. EASY TO CHECK.

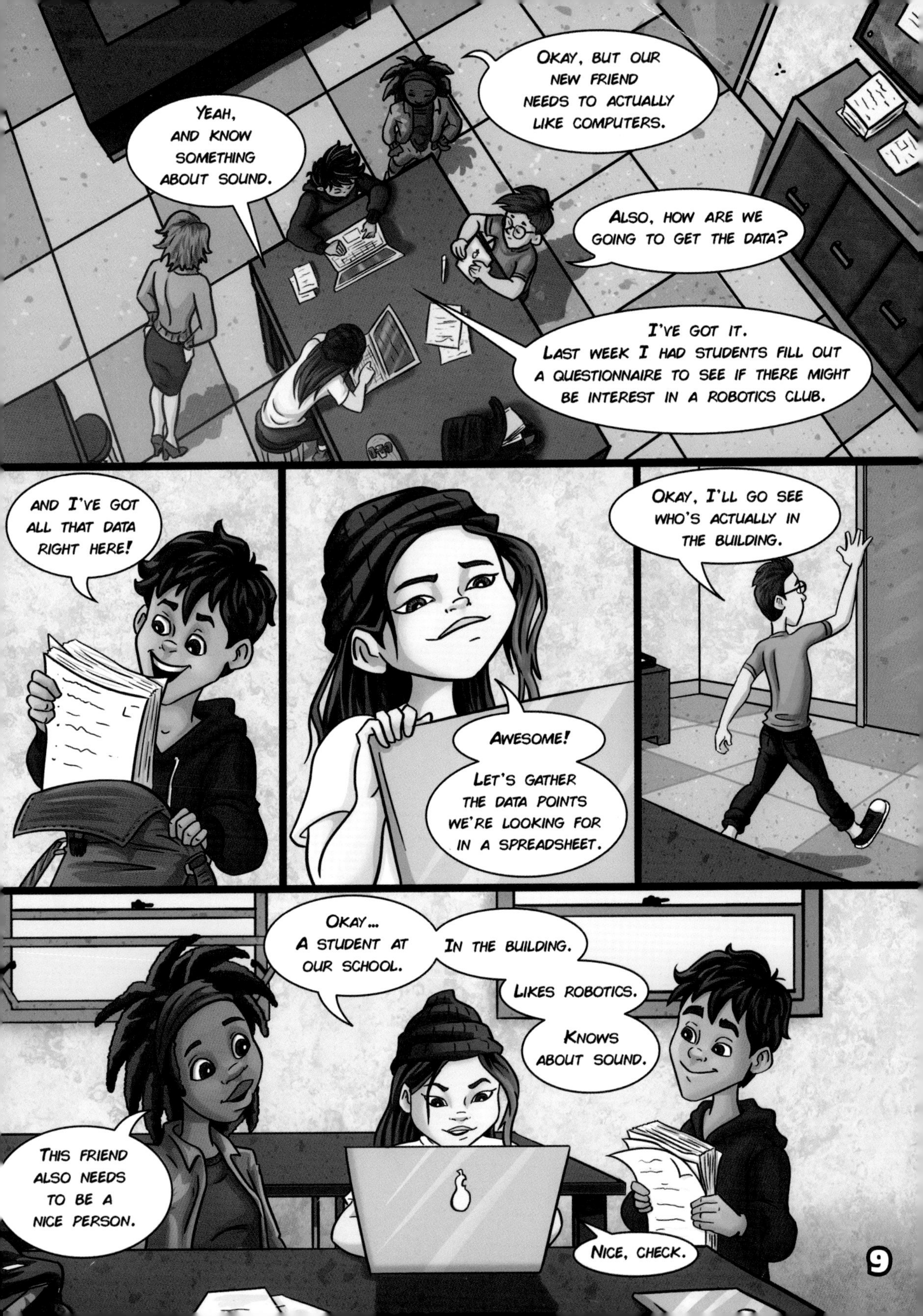
OKAY, BUT OUR NEW FRIEND NEEDS TO ACTUALLY LIKE COMPUTERS.
YEAH, AND KNOW SOMETHING ABOUT SOUND.
ALSO, HOW ARE WE GOING TO GET THE DATA?
I'VE GOT IT. LAST WEEK I HAD STUDENTS FILL OUT A QUESTIONNAIRE TO SEE IF THERE MIGHT BE INTEREST IN A ROBOTICS CLUB.
AND I'VE GOT ALL THAT DATA RIGHT HERE!
AWESOME!
LET'S GATHER THE DATA POINTS WE'RE LOOKING FOR IN A SPREADSHEET.
OKAY, I'LL GO SEE WHO'S ACTUALLY IN THE BUILDING.
OKAY... A STUDENT AT OUR SCHOOL.
IN THE BUILDING.
LIKES ROBOTICS.
KNOWS ABOUT SOUND.
THIS FRIEND ALSO NEEDS TO BE A NICE PERSON.
NICE, CHECK.

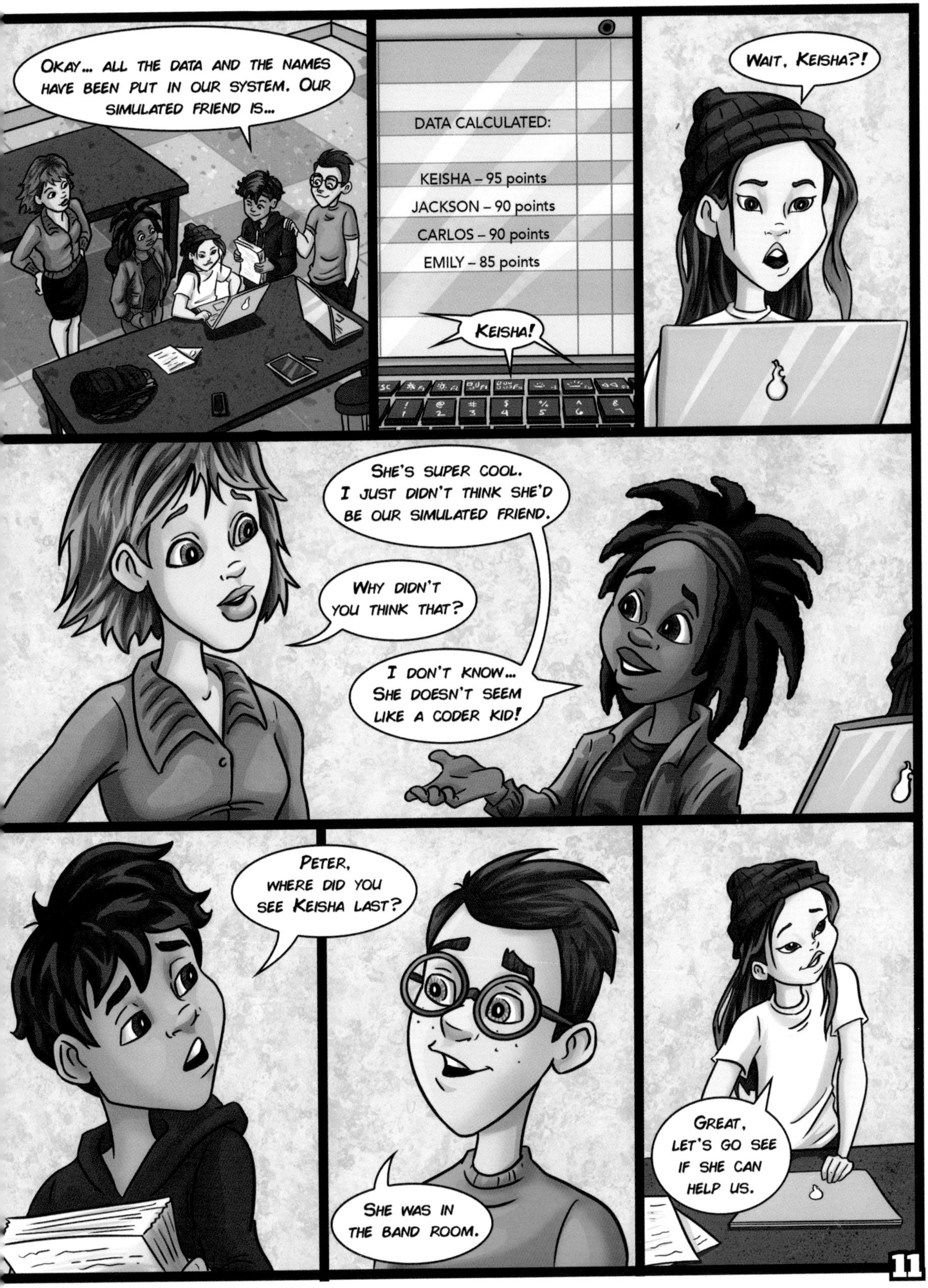
OKAY... ALL THE DATA AND THE NAMES HAVE BEEN PUT IN OUR SYSTEM. OUR SIMULATED FRIEND IS...
DATA CALCULATED:
KEISHA – 95 points
JACKSON – 90 points
CARLOS – 90 points
EMILY – 85 points
KEISHA!
WAIT, KEISHA?!
SHE'S SUPER COOL. I JUST DIDN'T THINK SHE'D BE OUR SIMULATED FRIEND.
WHY DIDN'T YOU THINK THAT?
I DON'T KNOW... SHE DOESN'T SEEM LIKE A CODER KID!
PETER, WHERE DID YOU SEE KEISHA LAST?
SHE WAS IN THE BAND ROOM.
GREAT, LET'S GO SEE IF SHE CAN HELP US.

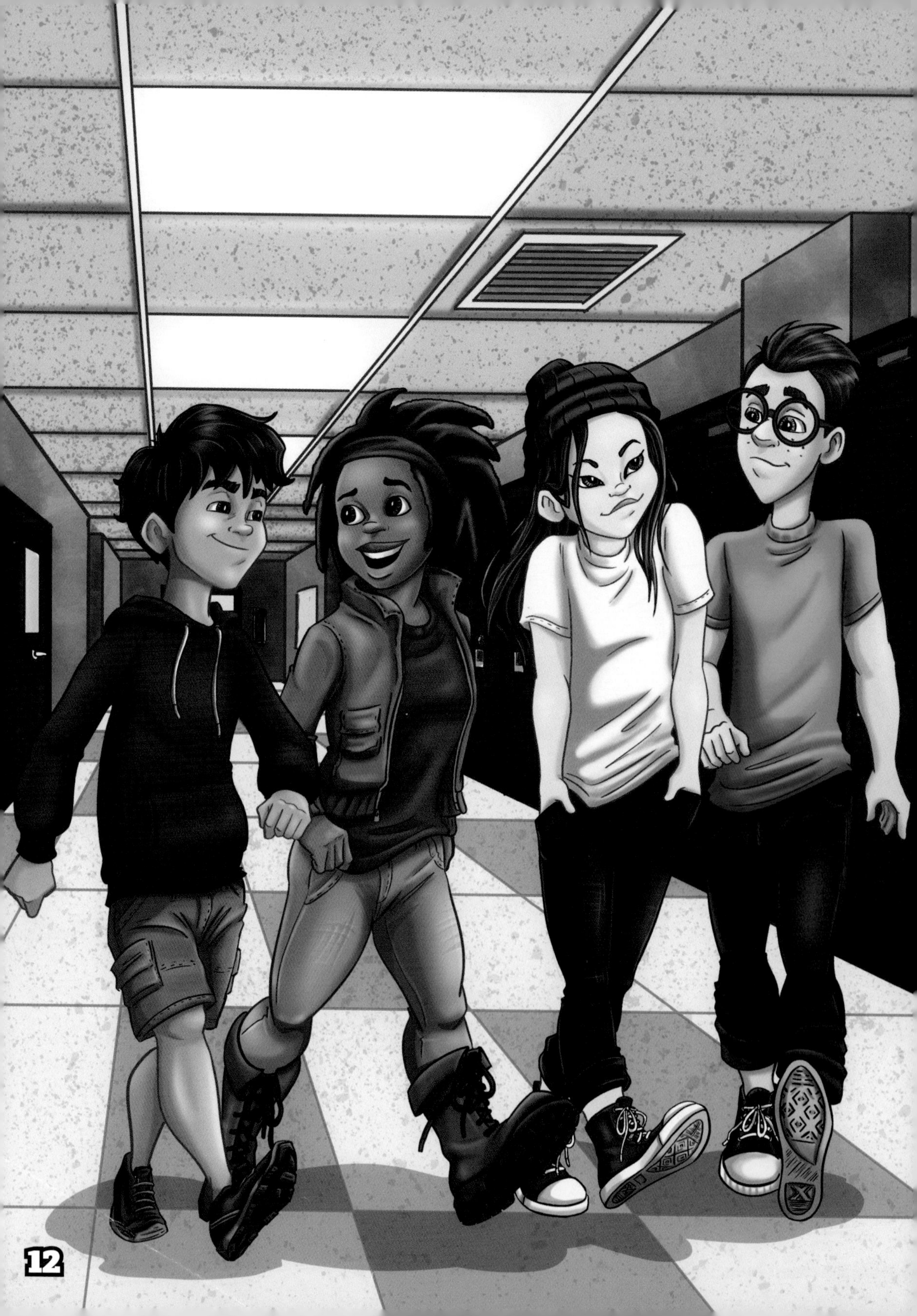

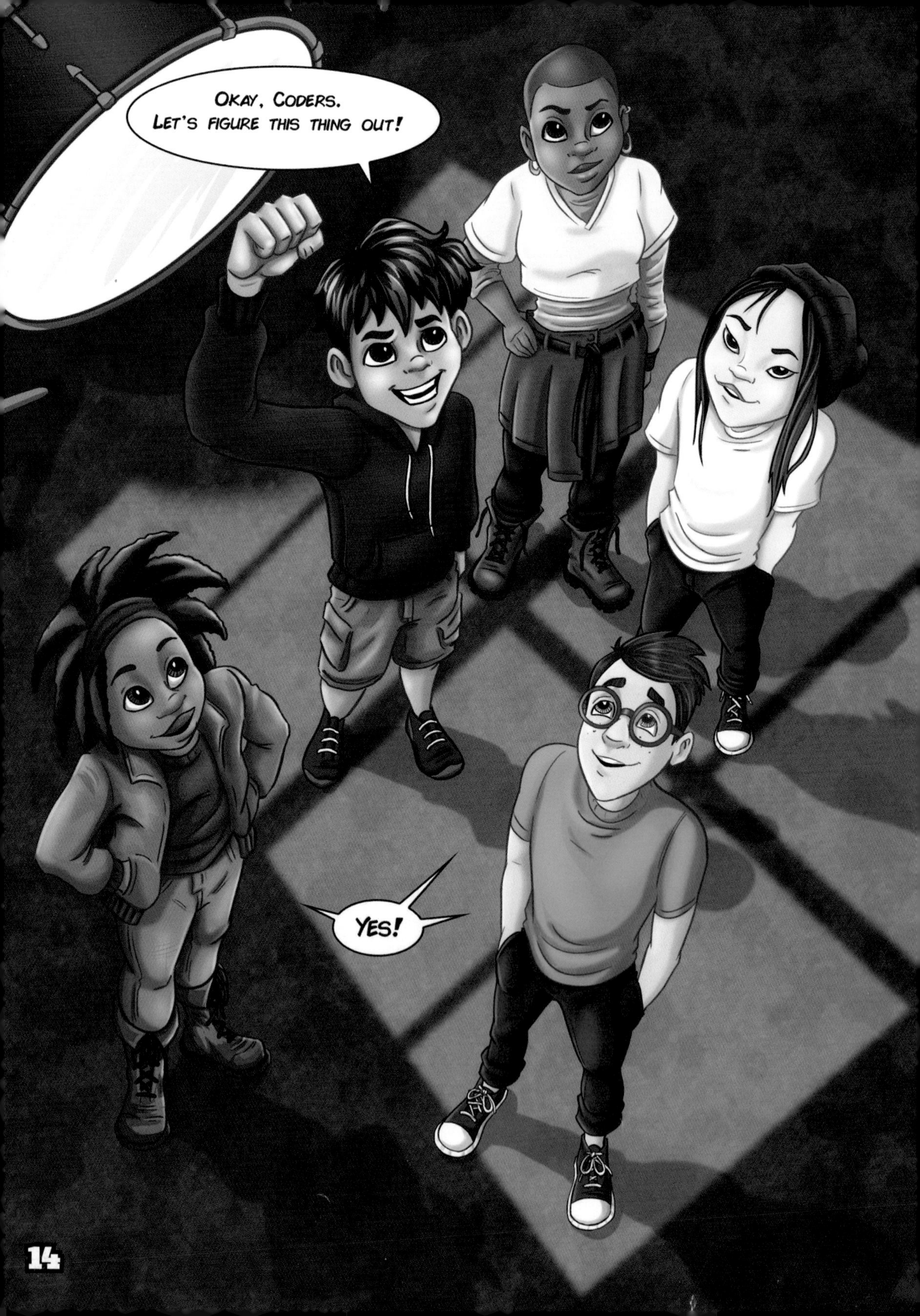
OKAY, CODERS.
LET'S FIGURE THIS THING OUT!
YES!

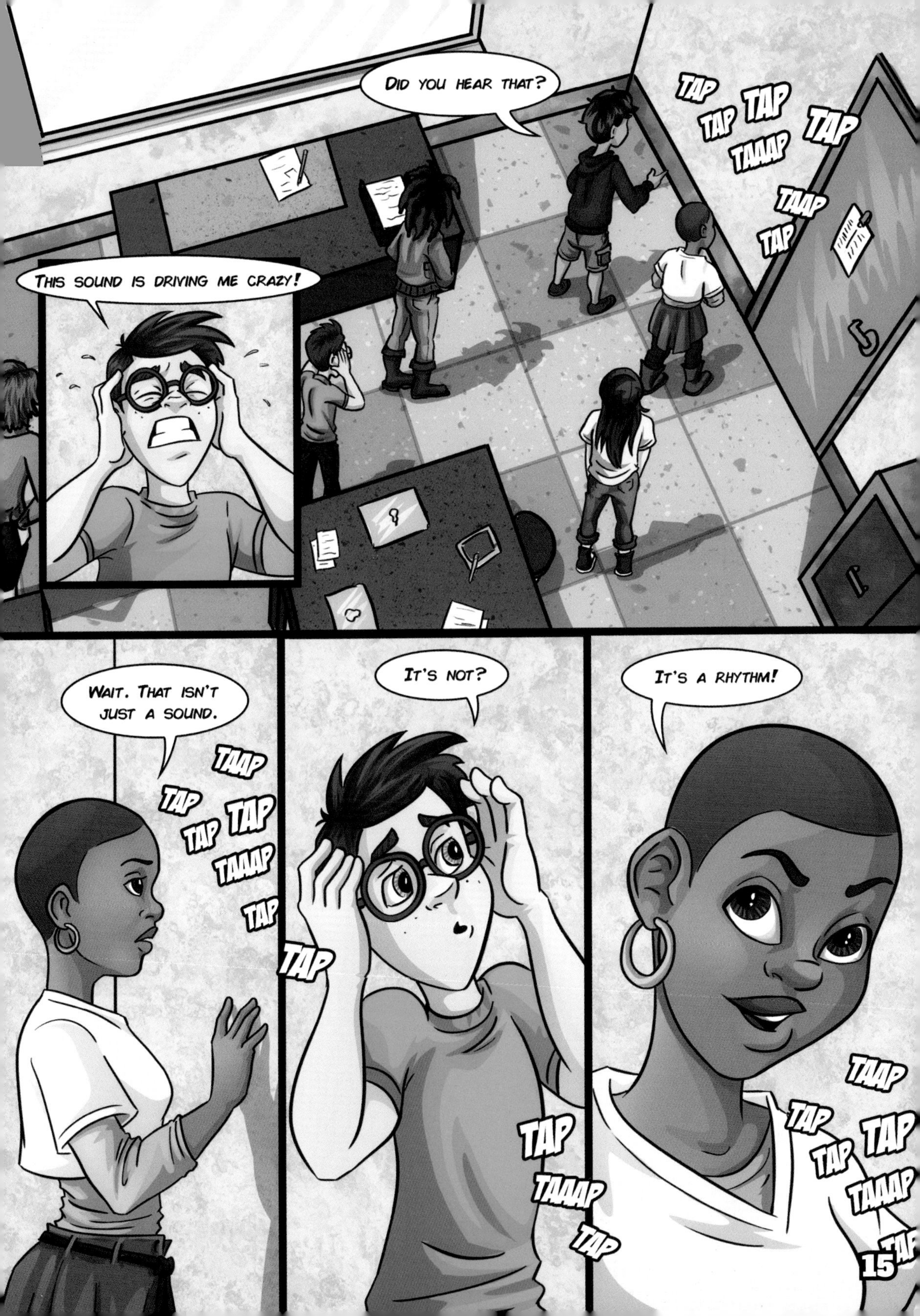
DID YOU HEAR THAT?
TAP TAP TAP TAP TAAAP TAAP TAP
THIS SOUND IS DRIVING ME CRAZY!
WAIT. THAT ISN'T JUST A SOUND.
TAAP TAP TAP TAP TAAAP TAP
IT'S NOT?
TAP TAP TAAAP TAP
IT'S A RHYTHM!
TAAP TAP TAP TAP TAAAP

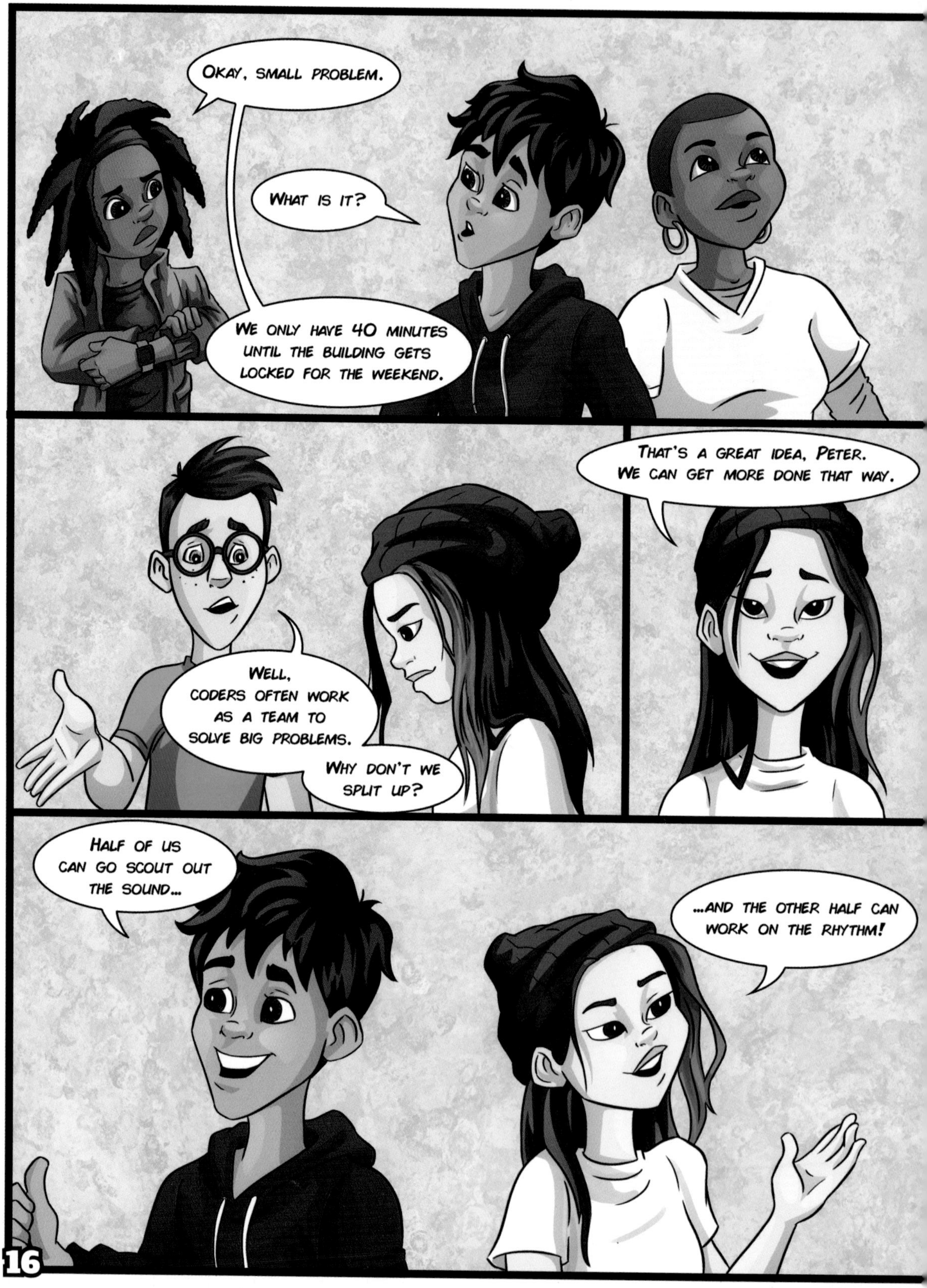

OKAY, SMALL PROBLEM.
WHAT IS IT?
WE ONLY HAVE 40 MINUTES UNTIL THE BUILDING GETS LOCKED FOR THE WEEKEND.
WELL, CODERS OFTEN WORK AS A TEAM TO SOLVE BIG PROBLEMS.
WHY DON'T WE SPLIT UP?
THAT'S A GREAT IDEA, PETER. WE CAN GET MORE DONE THAT WAY.
HALF OF US CAN GO SCOUT OUT THE SOUND...
...AND THE OTHER HALF CAN WORK ON THE RHYTHM!

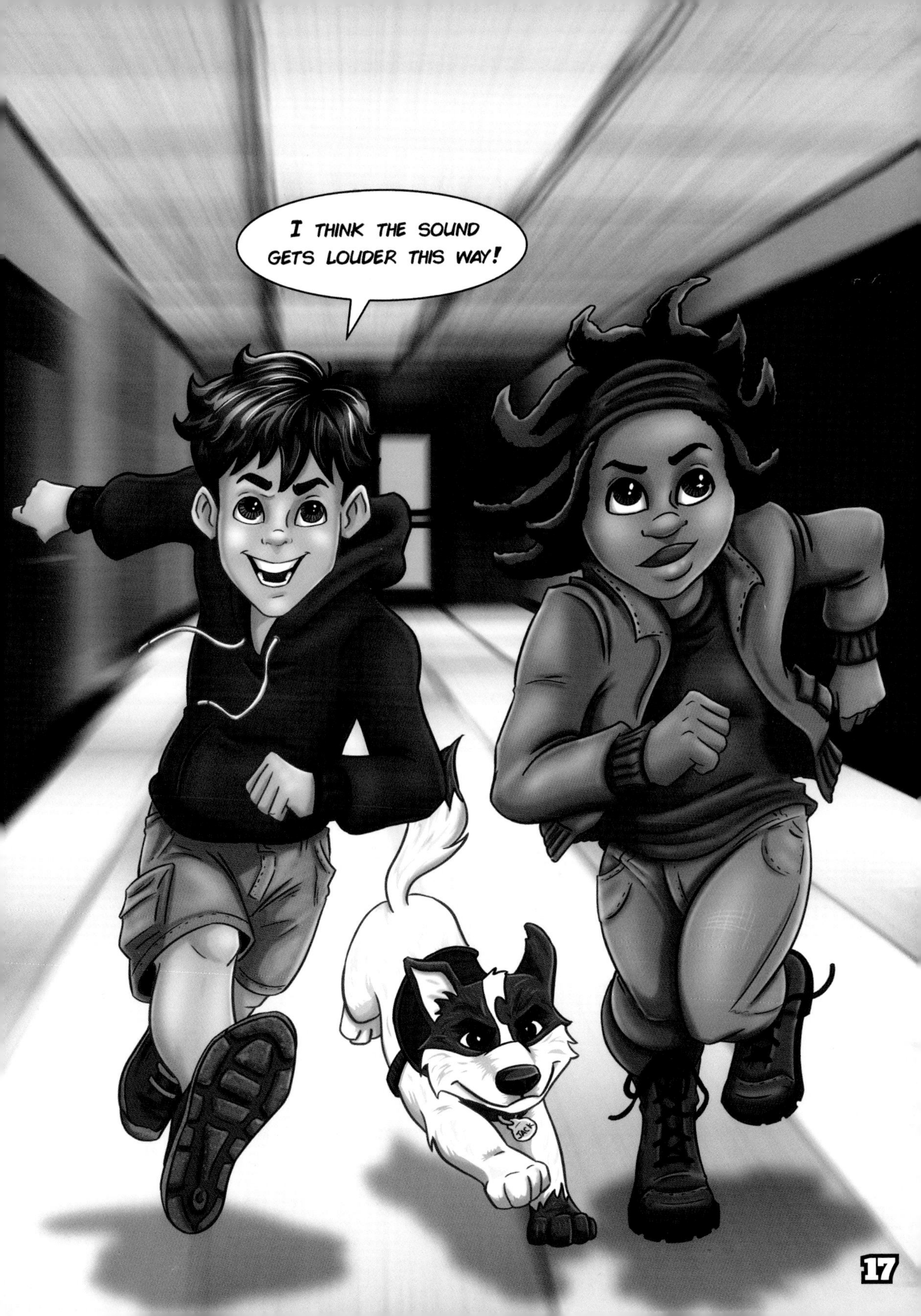
I THINK THE SOUND GETS LOUDER THIS WAY!
JACK

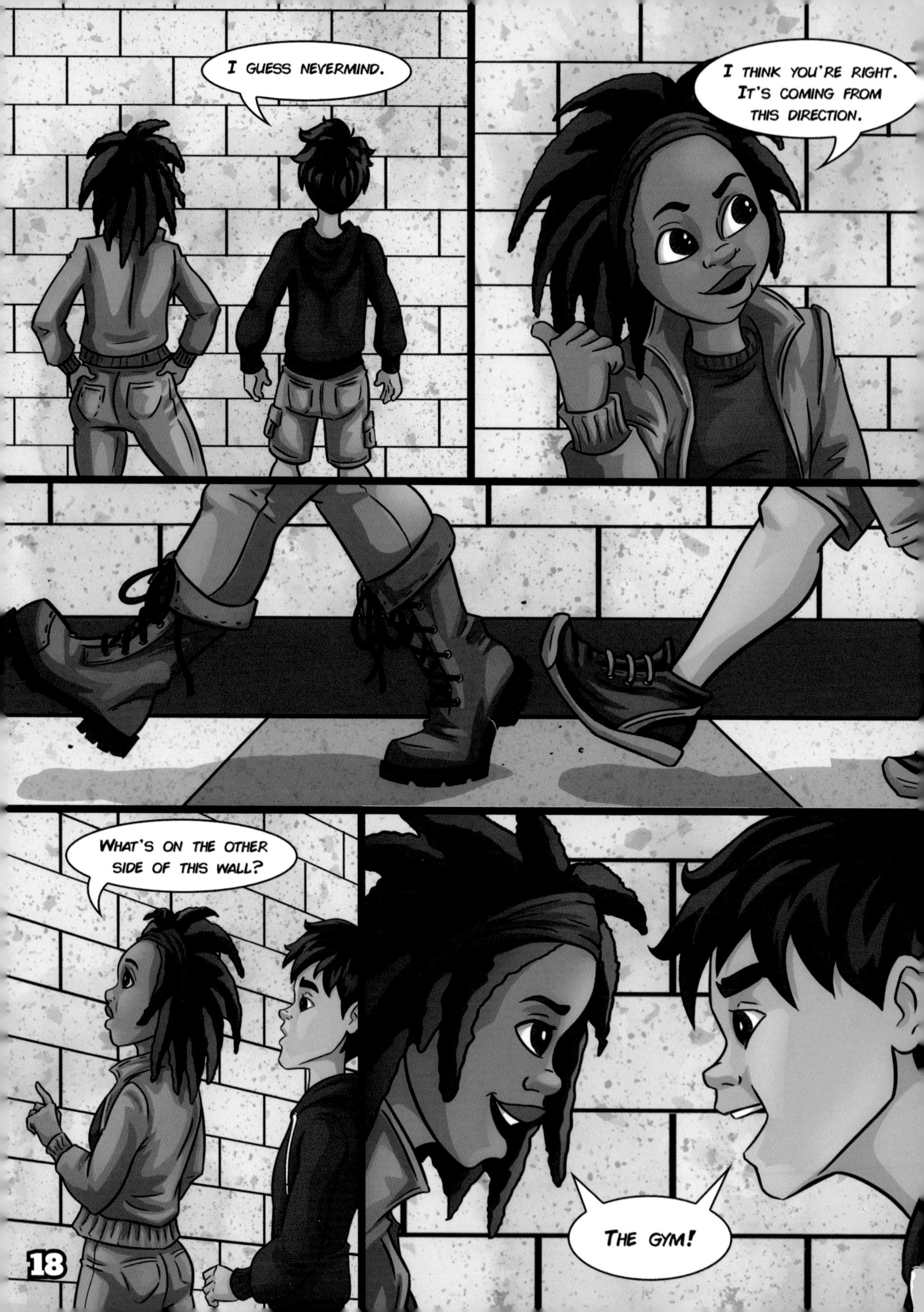

I GUESS NEVERMIND.
I THINK YOU'RE RIGHT. IT'S COMING FROM THIS DIRECTION.
WHAT'S ON THE OTHER SIDE OF THIS WALL?
THE GYM!

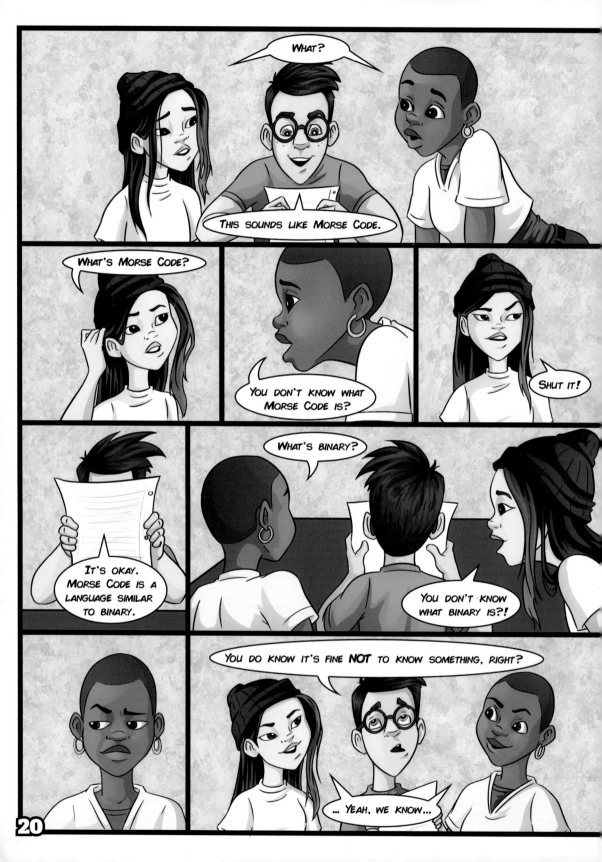

25

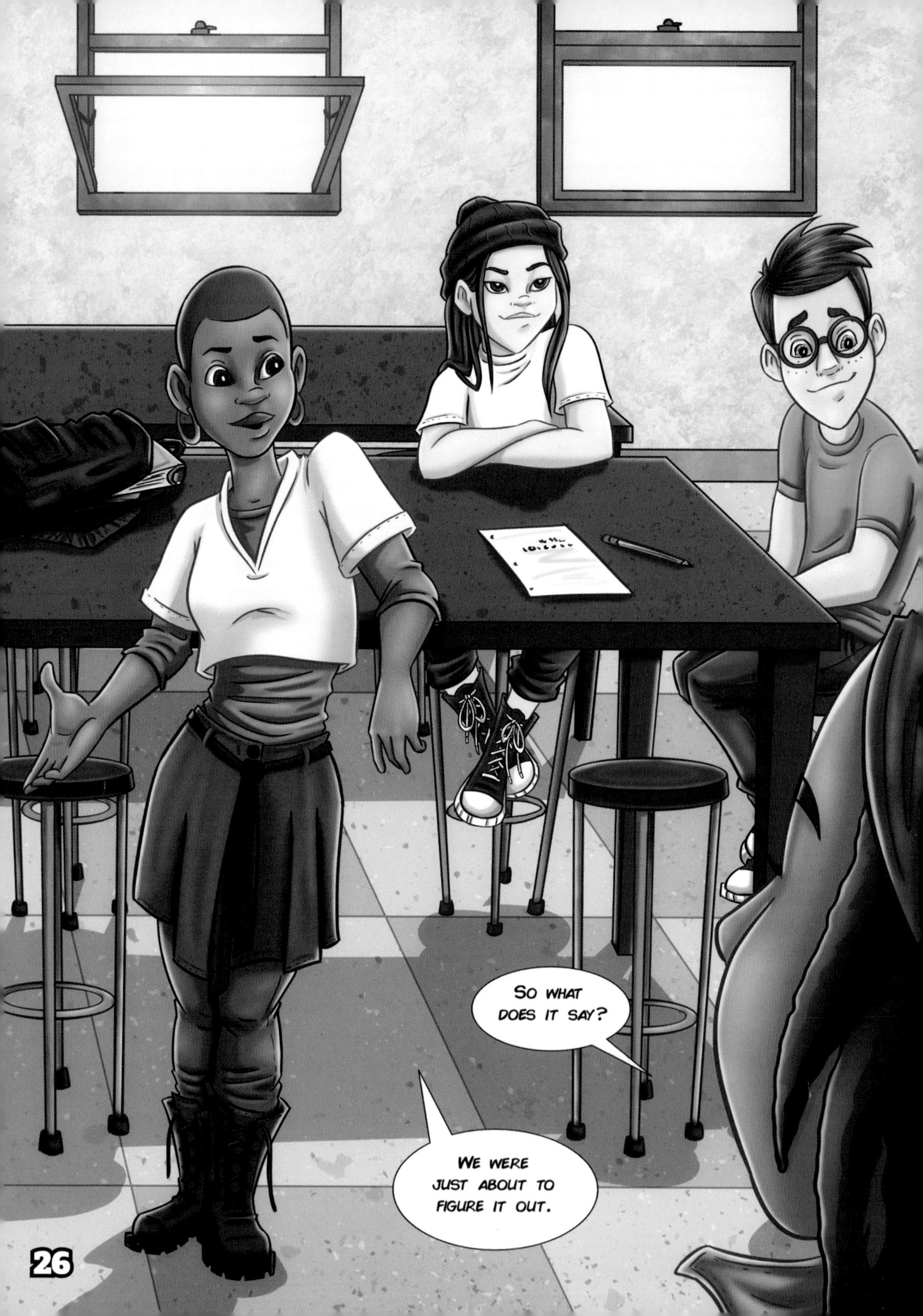
SO WHAT DOES IT SAY?
WE WERE JUST ABOUT TO FIGURE IT OUT.

A	●—	J	●———	S	●●●
B	—●●●	K	—●—	T	—
C	—●—●	L	●—●●	U	●●—
D	—●●	M	——	V	●●●—
E	●	N	—●	W	●——
F	●●—●	O	———	X	—●●—
G	——●	P	●——●	Y	—●——
H	●●●●	Q	——●—	Z	——●●
I	●●	R	●—●		

29